Paddington Bear
and the Christmas Surprise

MICHAEL BOND

Pictures by R. W. ALLEY

Weekly Reader is a registered trademark of Weekly Reader Corporation.

2002 Edition

 HarperCollins*Publishers*

Paddington Bear and the Christmas Surprise
Text copyright © 1997 by Michael Bond. Illustrations copyright © 1997 by HarperCollins Publishers.
Printed in the United States of America.
Library of Congress catalog card number: 96-14362
ISBN 0-06-027766-1. — ISBN 0-06-443595-4 (pbk.)
❖ http://www.harperchildrens.com

One Christmas Paddington announced he was taking the Brown family to Barkridges store to see Santa Claus.

"It's very good value," he explained. "Apart from meeting Mr. Claus, there's a sleigh ride through Winter

Wonderland and you get to visit his workshop at the North Pole. We might even see where he makes his marmalade."

"I doubt if Santa makes his own marmalade," said Mrs. Brown nervously, as Paddington led the way onto the escalator.

"It would make all the presents sticky," agreed Jonathan.

"Not to mention his beard," added Judy. "Besides, he's much too busy."

"That's more than you can say for Barkridges," remarked Mr. Brown gloomily, as he brought up the rear. "There's hardly anyone here."

There were two signs at the top of the escalator,
one pointing to Santa Claus, and one pointing to Winter
Wonderland.

"I think I may visit Santa Claus first," announced
Paddington, "in case the sleigh gets stuck in the snow."

"You're supposed to do it
the other way round, dear,"
called Mrs. Brown. "You
don't want to miss the ride."

But Paddington was already in line.

There were only two children in front of him and they were both rather large, so he got down on his paws and knees so that he could get a better look.

Santa Claus had two sacks of presents. One was marked BOYS and the other was marked GIRLS, but he couldn't see a sack marked BEARS anywhere.

Just then he looked up and saw
a man staring down at him.

"Are you a boy or are you a girl?" asked
the store manager.

"I'm neither," said Paddington. "I'm a bear."

"You look more like a large creepy-crawly
to me," said the man distastefully. "Perhaps you had better
come back next year when you've made up your mind."

"Come back next year," repeated
Paddington hotly. "But I've brought my
Christmas list. I thought it would save
the postage."

The Browns were too far away to hear what was being said, but from the look on Paddington's face they guessed something must be wrong.

"Hurry up," called Mrs. Bird. "We're all ready to go."

"Oh dear, Henry," said Mrs. Brown. "I do hope the sleigh ride is a success. Paddington's been saving his bun money for ages and he'll be most upset if it doesn't live up to his expectations."

As Paddington clambered aboard and they set off, Mr. Brown held up a leaflet. "Listen everybody," he called. "First of all, we go past Santa's winter garden."

"I think I prefer Mrs. Bird's window box," said Paddington.

The Browns exchanged anxious glances. It didn't seem a very good start to the outing.

"How about this one, then?" continued Mr. Brown, as they turned a corner. "It's the stable where Santa keeps his reindeer."

Paddington didn't say anything. From where he was sitting it looked more like a dog kennel, and the only reindeer he could see was a plastic one that had fallen over in the snow.

Next, Mr. Brown pointed to a very tall tower with a flashing light at the top. "That's the lighthouse at the North Pole," he said. "It's there to make sure Santa arrives back home safe and sound after he's delivered all his presents."

Paddington gave it a hard stare. "I think there must be a wire loose, Mr. Brown," he exclaimed. "The light keeps going on and off."

"Lighthouses are supposed to flash," broke in Jonathan. "They all send out a different signal so that people know exactly where they are."

But Paddington wasn't listening. He was counting the number of buns it had taken to pay for the outing.

"Now, this might be more interesting." Mr. Brown tried to strike a cheerful note as they drew nearer to a big house with mechanical figures moving behind every window. "We're about to enter Santa's workshop."

"Look at all the elves," called Judy.

She turned around in order to explain elves to Paddington, but as she did so she gave a cry of alarm, for he was nowhere to be seen.

"Do something, Henry!" cried Mrs. Brown when she saw what had happened.

"Do something?" repeated Mr. Brown. "What can I do from inside the middle of a workshop?"

"We haven't reached the end of the tour," warned Mrs. Bird. "Paddington will be most upset if he misses any of it."

Mr. Brown tried to put a brave face on things, but when they reached the end of the ride and there was still no sign of Paddington he looked as worried as any of them.

He called to one of Santa's helpers.

"There's a bear fallen into our works?" repeated the man. "I'll send for the manager at once!"

"Bear?" exclaimed the manager. "Did I hear someone say bear? If it's the one I met earlier, I'm not surprised he's missing. A troublemaker if ever I saw one. Blue duffel coat . . . old hat. I'd recognize him anywhere. Leave it to me—I'll find him."

"We're certainly not going until you have," warned Mrs. Bird. "And what's more, if I know that bear he'll be wanting his money back."

"No one has *ever* asked for their money back before," wailed the manager.

"There's a first time for everything," said Mrs. Bird grimly.

As the manager disappeared through one door, Paddington came through another.

"I think I've found the fault in the lighthouse, Mr. Brown," he called. "Bears are good at mending things and . . ."

But before he had a chance to finish there was a loud bang from somewhere inside Santa's workshop, and all the lights went out.

"Where is he?" shouted the manager. "Where is he? I'll give him a present he won't forget in a hurry!"

Mrs. Bird took a firm grip of her umbrella.

"Come along, everyone," she called. "I think we've had enough wonders for one day."

"Paddington's certainly hit the headlines," said Mr. Brown at breakfast the next morning. "Listen to this: 'Strange Goings-on in London Store'."

"One thing's certain," said Mrs. Brown. "We shan't be allowed into Barkridges again in a hurry."

"I don't know," broke in Jonathan. "Listen to this one: 'Crowds Flock to Santa's Workshop. Search for Mystery Bear Goes On'."

Everyone was so busy reading the newspapers that they didn't notice Mrs. Bird leave the room. She had an important telephone call to make.

"Barkridges," said the manager, several days later, "wishes you all a very Merry Christmas. Ever since this young bear first honored us with a visit we've had lines all around our store. It's quite like old times."

He turned to Mrs. Bird. "And thank you, dear lady, for telephoning us when you did."

"Perhaps I could do some more repairs for you?" said Paddington hopefully.

"I don't think that will be necessary," said the manager hastily. "Besides, Santa is waiting to see you. *After* you've all had a free sleigh ride."

It was a merry party of Browns who set off on their journey through Winter Wonderland. This time everything worked perfectly, and when they came to the end of the ride Santa Claus was waiting to greet them.

"Ho ho ho," he boomed. "And who have we here?"

"I'm a bear, Mr. Claus," said Paddington. "And I come from Darkest Peru."

"Well," said Santa, reaching behind his chair, "in that case I think I know just what you would like."

Paddington nearly fell over backwards with surprise as Santa Claus held up an enormous jar. There was a label on the side that said HOMEMADE and it was tied at the top with a big red bow.

"It's my favorite, Mr. Claus!" he cried. "How did you guess?"

Mrs. Bird's face went pink as Santa gave her a knowing smile. "One of the nice things about Santa Claus," she said hastily, "is that he knows exactly what everyone wants for Christmas. That's what makes him so special."

"*And* he makes his own marmalade," said Paddington happily. "I knew he would!"